OBRIEN

panda series

PANDA books are for first readers
beginning to make their own way
through books.

Katie's Cake

STEPHANIE DAGG

• Pictures by Stephen Hall •

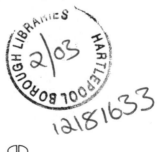

THE O'BRIEN PRESS
DUBLIN

First published 1999 by The O'Brien Press Ltd.,
20 Victoria Road, Dublin 6, Ireland.
Tel: +353 1 4923333; Fax: +353 1 4922777
E-mail: books@obrien.ie
Website: www.obrien.ie
Reprinted 1999, 2002.

ISBN: 0-86278-617-7

British Library Cataloguing-in-Publication Data
Dagg, Stephanie
Katie's Cake. - (O'Brien pandas)
1. Children's stories
I. Title
823.9'14 [J]

3   4   5   6   7   8   9   10
02   03   04   05   06

The O'Brien Press receives
assistance from

The Arts Council
An Chomhairle Ealaíon

Typesetting, layout, editing, design: The O'Brien Press Ltd.
Cover separations: C&A Print Services Ltd.
Printing: Cox & Wyman Ltd.

Can YOU spot the panda
hidden in the story?

'Wow! Cool cake, Mum!'
said Katie.
Mum had made a birthday
cake for Auntie Susan.
Auntie Susan
was coming to tea.

Mum covered the cake
with lots of icing –
all the colours
of the rainbow.

Mum smiled proudly.
'It's a rainbow cake,' she said.
'Now, I'm going to have
a cup of tea and
watch television.
Are you coming, Katie?'

'No way,' replied Katie rudely.
'I hate that quiz you watch.
I'll play in here.'

'Okay,' said Mum, 'but
don't touch the cake.'

'I won't,' promised Katie.
And she didn't.

Well, not for **five minutes**.

But the icing looked so nice
that after **six minutes**
she had to have some.

Katie poked a finger
into the stripe of blue icing
and tasted it.

'Yum!' she said.
'Delicious!
I wonder if the other colours
taste as nice.'

So she sampled each one.
First the **red**, then the **yellow**,
then the **green**.
They were all delicious.
It was hard to tell
which was best,
so she tried each colour
again.

And **again**.

And **again**.

And **again**.

The icing was so nice
that Katie didn't notice
how much she was eating.

Then she put out her finger
for one last lick
and touched

bare cake.

The icing was all gone!
Katie looked at the cake.
'Oh no!' she gasped.
'It's ruined.
What'll I do?'

The mixing bowl
was still on the table.
Katie looked in.

There was some
yellow icing still in it.

But there wasn't
very much.
'I'll have to make more!'
said Katie.

But how?

How do you make icing?

Katie thought for a minute.

She knew that icing
had lots of **sugar** in it
because Mum always said
it was bad for your teeth.

She thought it had
butter in it too.
But what else?

If it's called icing, she thought,
it must have **ice** in it,
mustn't it?

There was some
butter and sugar still
on the table,
so Katie popped those into
the mixing bowl.

Next she went to the freezer
and pulled the
heavy door open.
She looked in.

There were no ice-cubes,
but Katie found
a tub of **ice-cream**.
'That will have to do!'
she said.

She took it to the table
(licking it a few times)
and dropped it into
the mixing bowl.

Then she pounded away
at the mixture
with a wooden spoon.
'Gosh! This is hard work!'
she panted.
She stopped for a rest.

She looked into the bowl.
It was full of
lumpy, **bumpy**,
yukky yellow stuff.

Katie shrugged.

It was the best she could do.

She took a couple of handfuls
of her mixture
and smeared it on the
bare cake.

But it all slid off again!

Katie scooped it up
and plastered it back on.
Again it slid off.

'It's too runny,'
said Katie.
'Now, Mum always puts
flour in her cooking
when it's too runny.
I'll have to get some flour!'

She rummaged through
the food cupboard
until she found
a big bag of flour
at the back.

Just to be on the safe side,
she poured all of it
into the bowl.
She began to mix again.

After about three stirs,
the icing became **so solid**
she couldn't move the spoon
any more.
'Oh no!' wailed Katie.
She was starting to panic.

Mum's quiz would be over soon
and she'd come into the kitchen
and find this mess!

And Auntie Susan would
be here any minute!

Katie was desperate.

'I'll put some **water**
into the icing,'
she muttered.

But she couldn't reach
the kitchen tap,
even when she stood
on a chair.

Then she saw some
washing-up water
in the sink.
It was only a tiny bit frothy
and a teensy bit dirty.

'That'll do,'
said Katie.
She scooped up a mugful
and added it to her mixture.

She attacked it
with the wooden spoon again.
After a few minutes,
the icing looked
much better.

This time when Katie
plastered it on to the cake,
it **stuck firmly**.
The cake was soon covered.

Now there were just
the rainbow colours
to sort out.

'I'll need my **paintbox**
for that,'
decided Katie.

She got her paintbox
from the cupboard
and set to work.

The paintbrush kept getting
clogged up with icing.
Katie had to use
an awful lot of paint.
But at last she was finished.

The cake looked ... well ...
almost as good as new.

Just then the doorbell rang.
It was Auntie Susan.
Mum opened the door.
'Happy birthday, Susan,'
she said. 'We have a
nice surprise for you
in the kitchen.'

They came into the kitchen.

'Hello, Katie,' said Auntie Susan. 'Busy painting? And what a **lovely birthday cake**! I can't wait to have a slice!'

Katie managed a tiny smile.

'Happy birthday, Auntie Susan,'

she whispered.

Mum cut a big slice of cake.
She put it on a plate
for Auntie Susan.

'Oh no!' said Auntie Susan.
'That's much too big for me.
Katie must have that slice.
Here you are, love!'

She passed the slice of cake
to Katie.

Katie gulped.

She looked at Mum.

She looked at Auntie Susan.

They were both smiling
at her,
waiting for her
to take a bite.

Katie closed her eyes ...

... and sank her teeth in!

Yuck!

It tasted disgusting.

It tasted **horrible**.

It tasted **revolting**.

But Katie bravely
swallowed it down.

'Lovely!' she croaked.
She opened her eyes.

Mum and Auntie Susan,
were chewing away.
Blue paint dribbled
down their chins.

They were looking
at each other
in horror.
Then they looked
at Katie.

But Katie was running,
as fast as her legs
could carry her ...